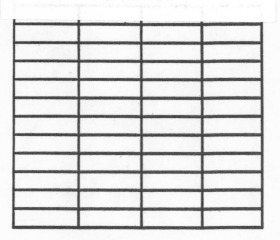

D1413987

Waiting for Jennifer

Waiting for Jennifer

Kathryn Osebold Galbraith
illustrated by Irene Trivas

Margaret K. McElderry Books
NEW YORK

Margaret K. McElderry Books
Macmillan Publishing Company
866 Third Avenue
New York, NY 10022
Collier Macmillan Canada, Inc.

Composition by Boro Typographers, Inc.
New York, New York
Printed and bound in Japan by Toppan Printing Co.

First Edition
Printed in the United States of America
10 9 8 7 6 5 4 3 2 1

Library of Congress Cataloging-in-Publication Data

Galbraith, Kathryn Osebold.
Waiting for Jennifer.

Summary: Nan and Thea eagerly await the arrival
of a new baby in their family, confident that it will
be a girl.
[1. Babies—Fiction.   2. Brothers and sisters—
Fiction] I. Trivas, Irene, ill.   II. Title.
PZ7.G1303Wai 1987   [E]   87-4151
ISBN 0-689-50430-6

The original illustrations for Waiting for Jennifer are
colored pencil and pen and ink.

"I have a secret to tell you," Mama said.

Nan and Thea squeezed onto Mama's lap to hear.

"There's going to be a new baby in the house," she whispered.

"A new baby! When?"

"Not for a while," Mama said. "It takes nine whole months before a baby is ready to be born. We have six months left to wait."

Thea thought they should call the new baby Bridget, but Nan said, "No, 'Jennifer' is prettier. Besides, I already know how to spell it."

"Maybe we should think of some boys' names too," Mama said gently.

Nan shook her head. "Oh, no. We want a sister. A little sister named Jennifer."

Nan told Patrick and Isabel about Jennifer. She told the mailman and Mr. Feinstein who lived next door.

"I'm going to be a bigger sister," she told all the children in Miss Newcomb's room. "I'm Thea's big sister, and now I'm going to be Jennifer's."

"We're having a baby!" Thea whispered to Chessie. "Now I'm going to be a big sister too!"

For Halloween Nan decided to be a princess with a tinfoil crown. Thea decided to be a frog. She dressed all in green and wore her sister's rubber flippers. Mama took them from house to house. She wore a big sweatshirt that said BABY across the front.

"When is Jennifer coming?" Patrick and Isabel asked. Mr. Feinstein asked the same thing.

"Not for a while," Mama told them all. "Babies take a long time. We still have five more months to wait."

Auntie Nor and Uncle William came for Thanksgiving. Nan and Thea helped Daddy set the table. Daddy counted out six white china plates and six white napkins. "Just think," he said, "next Thanksgiving there'll be seven."

"Oh, quick!" Mama said. She put their hands on her stomach. "Feel that? There! That's the baby!"

Santa brought a sled with red runners for Christmas. He also brought furry earmuffs for Nan, bunny slippers for Thea, and a green sweater for Daddy. For Mama, Santa brought a new dress. A big bright yellow one. Mama was so pleased, she put it right on. "Now *this* should last until the baby comes."

Nan forgot to take her new earmuffs for show-and-tell. Instead, she told Miss Newcomb and her first-grade class about Jennifer again.

"Did your mom have two babies?" asked Holly. "Or is this the same old one?"

When Nan came home from school that day, she said, "Everybody is tired of waiting. Isn't Jennifer ever going to come?"

In Miss Newcomb's class Nan painted a picture of George Washington's cherry tree. Mama put it up on the refrigerator. Thea painted a picture of an apple tree. Mama taped it up right beside Nan's.

"Guess what we're going to paint on Saturday?" Daddy said. "The baby's room!" Before Nan and Thea could ask, he added, "It won't be too long now."

Nan and Thea sat on Mama's bed and watched her pack her suitcase. "Just in case," Mama said. "I want to be ready when the baby comes."

Into the suitcase along with Mama's blue-flowered nightie went the picture of Daddy with Nan and Thea from the top of the dresser.

Thea drew Mama a picture of Chessie to take to the hospital too. "So you won't be too lonesome," she said.

Nan and Thea went to bed early that night. It was hard to fall asleep. "Maybe tonight Jennifer will come!" But in the morning Mama said, "No, not yet."

"No, not yet," Mama told the mailman and Mr. Feinstein and Patrick and Isabel. "No, not yet."

"Nan," Mama said. "Would you please hand me my shoes?"
"Thea, honey, would you please pick up my book?"
Mama sighed. "I don't think this baby is ever going to come."

"Now it's time," Mama whispered. She woke Nan and Thea up with a kiss.

While Daddy waited with Mama in the hospital, Nan and Thea waited at home with Auntie Nor. And waited and waited. "I'm glad I gave her the picture of Chessie," Thea said.

Finally the telephone rang. "It's Daddy," Nan shouted.
"Has Jennifer really come?"
Daddy laughed. "Yes, the baby's here. But it's not Jennifer."
"It's not?"
"No, not unless you want to call your little brother Jenny."
"We have a brother? A baby brother!"

"But what are we going to call him?"

"'Tom' is a nice name," Thea said softly.

Nan thought a minute. "'Tom' *is* nice. Besides, I already know how to spell it!"